Bumble Bear
THE BEEGINNING

WRITTEN BY JAMES HOFFMAN ILLUSTRATED BY JOHN SANDFORD

Dedicated to one of my cubs,
Deborah Lynn.

J.D.H.

For Wes Smith,
my lifelong friend.

J.S.

Bear loved honey. He loved honey more than any other bear could imagine loving it. He and his family lived in a cozy, little cottage on Honey Hill Farm that had shelves for honey and jam. But the honey jars on the shelves were usually empty, because Bear ate honey all day long.

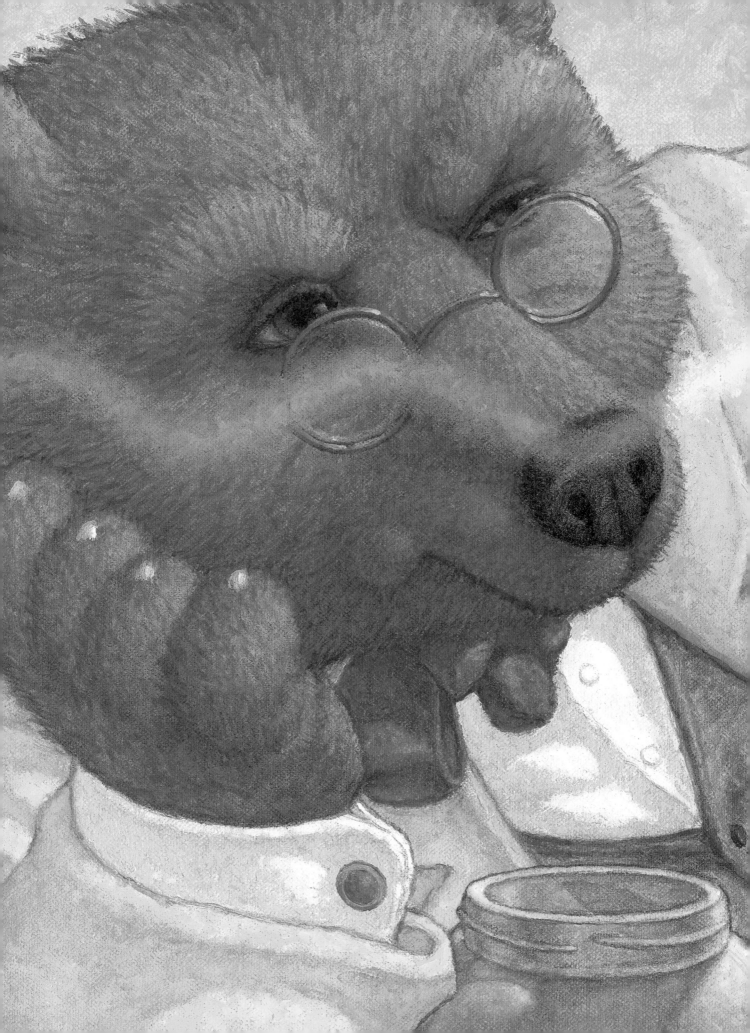

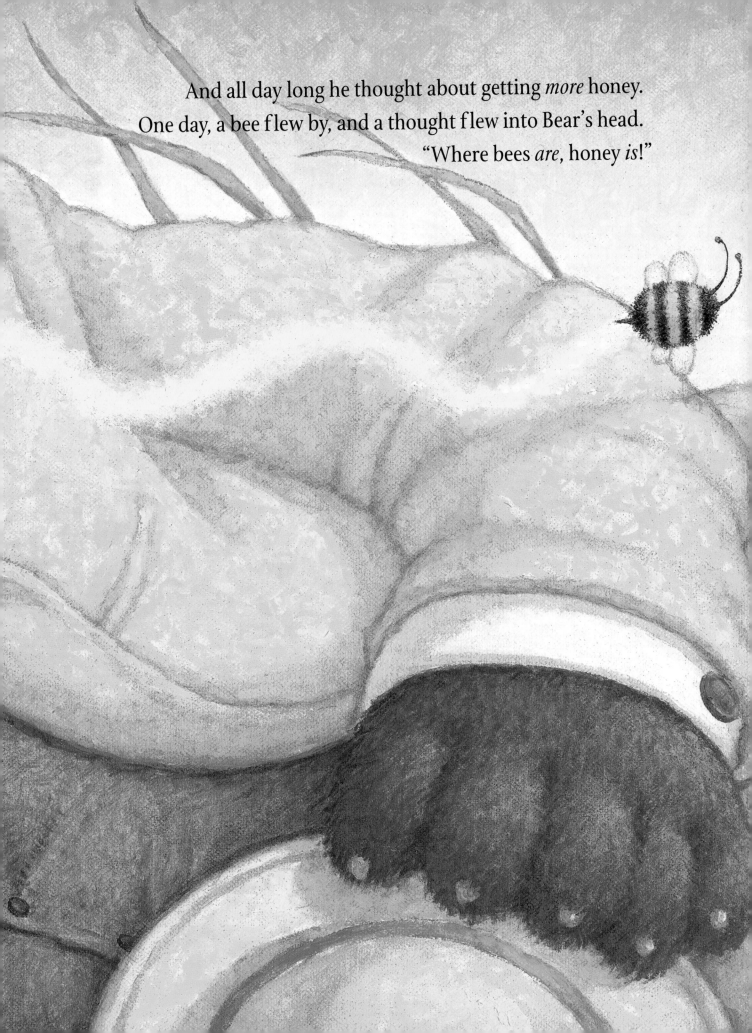

And all day long he thought about getting *more* honey.
One day, a bee flew by, and a thought flew into Bear's head.
"Where bees *are*, honey *is*!"

He followed the bee to its hive. Then another idea came to Bear. "To get closer to the hive — to get the honey — I can dress like a bee!"

He'd wear his striped pajamas! He'd hum a bee's buzz!
He'd pretend to fly! "And then, when the bees think I'm
just another big bee, I'll grab the honey!" he thought,
quickly changing clothes.

He finished his costume and spread his arms.
"I am Bumble Bear!" he shouted. And off he dashed to the beehive.

As soon as he saw the hive, Bumble Bear became much too eager to put his paws on the honey. He forgot to hum or pretend to fly. He even forgot he was dressed like a bee. He wanted the honey so badly he made a beeline straight to the hive, crashing through the field, making more noise than a freight train.

Bumble Bear was so close to the hive, he could imagine reaching right inside for the honey. Then he stumbled!

He tripped and tumbled!

He was *really* flying through the air now! He knocked over
the hive as he landed and combs of honey flew into
the air, just out of reach.

And something else flew toward
Bumble Bear—a swarm of angry bees.
Bumble Bear had truly bumbled!

The bees aimed straight for the place where Bumble Bear's homemade stinger *used* to be. He felt stungled! He jumped into the water to get away from the bees. As a *Bee*ginner, he hadn't even been able to get close to the honey in the hive.

When he landed in the pond, the cold water eased the hurt of his stings—but not his feelings. He'd lost his glasses. And he wore a hive on his head—a hive with no honey in it. "All this trouble and still no honey!" he thought. Bumble Bear had been humbled.

He grumbled as he trudged home in his underwear. Home to empty jars. Home to hungry Gwendolyn Bear, his wife, and his two cubs, Wear and Tear.

His stomach rumbled. It rumbled so loudly it scared the birds.
So loudly, in fact, that Wear and Tear and Gwendolyn Bear
heard him coming. They watched this rumbling and
grumbling from the cottage windows.

That night, Bumble Bear lectured to Wear and Tear on the value
of honey as he peered into the depths of an empty jar.
Wear and Tear and Gwendolyn Bear were used
to this lecture. They'd heard it all before.

After his speech, Bumble Bear went to his study and planned far into the night, thinking up new ways to get honey into his rumbling tummy.

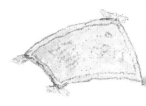

"Tomorrow I'll try again," he mumbled. "What if…"

Upstairs, Gwendolyn tucked the cubs into bed. Tear said,
"Daddy sure likes honey, but I like race cars."
"I like Pooh and honey, too,"
Wear said sleepily.

"I like a real honey,
and that's your father," said Gwendolyn Bear.
"He's a good bear but not a very good bee. Good night."